Dommy B has won New York's famous Nuyorican Poetry Cafe Slam and UK's Superheroes of Slam. He has performed his poetry on BBC's 'Rhyme Rocket'.

The Story of When Trolls Try to Eat Your Goldfish is adapted from his own poetry theatre show for children aged 5 plus and their families.

By Dommy B:

The Story of Spark, the Goblin Wizard

The Story of When Trolls Try to Eat Your Goldfish

THE STORY OF WHEN TROLLS TRY TO EAT YOUR GOLDFISH

DOMMY B

Flapjack Press
flapjackpress.co.uk

exploring the synergy between performance and the page

Published in 2014 by Flapjack Press
Chiffon Way, Salford, Gtr Manchester
flapjackpress.co.uk

dominicberry.net/trolls

ISBN 978-0-9576639-4-7

Cover, illustrations & puzzles by Brink
paulneads.co.uk

Printed by Lonsdale Direct
Denington Estate, Wellingborough, Northants
lonsdaledirect.co.uk

CONTENTS

Dedicated to Ian.
Thank you for being the greatest of friends
and always helping me face those trolls.

CHAPTER ONE

THE SEAGULLS KNOW WHAT IS REALLY BEING SAID

When the animals disappear, the first to go are the seagulls.

Can you speak Seagullese?

Anyone who can speak Seagullese knows that all seagulls want to do is please. You might think they screech and squall, but seagulls just like saying nice things. That's all. So, if you hear one call

CAW CAW CAW

what that seagull is really saying is,

"Why, hello there, Liam.
Your feathers look divine.
That shade of grey does suit you.
What do you think of mine?"

Seagullese always rhymes.

If a second seagull replies to the first,

"Noel! You charmer!
Your beak's so awfully neat.
You might admire my feathers but
I'd love to have your feet!"

if you didn't speak Seagullese, all you would hear is

CAW CAW CAW

but the seagulls know what is really being said.

CHAPTER TWO

A GIRL CALLED NIKKI

In a little, blue house by a bridge across a stream near a deep, dark forest, lives a young girl called Nikki.

When the seagulls disappear, Nikki is the first person to notice.

Nikki goes to ask her Mum if she knows where the seagulls have gone, but before Nikki can say anything, her Mum squeals,

"Look at my precious!
Is there anyone as pretty
as you, my little darling,
you're my one and only... Kitty."

Nikki's Mum points to where her cat is sat, one back leg raised in the air, quietly washing... its bottom.

Nikki has always wanted a pet of her own; perhaps a puppy, a pony or a python. Two months ago, Nikki's Mum said she was allowed any animal in the world, as long as that animal was... a goldfish.

Nikki's Mum said only goldfish were allowed because goldfish are *quiet* and Kitty is a very *sensitive* cat who needs her peace and quiet.

Nikki's Mum spends a lot of time looking after her vegetable patch. She is especially proud of her carrots.

Nikki likes it best when her Mum is outside, when not even Kitty's purr can be heard, when Nikki is upstairs with her goldfish...

Great Bumbleduke the Third.

He's not a cat. He's not a bird.
He is Great Bumbleduke the Third.
He's not got feathers. He's not furred.
He is Great Bumbleduke the Third.

You speak to him and you'll be heard,
heard by Great Bumbleduke the Third.
He never interrupts one word.
He is Great Bumbleduke the Third.

He listens
and... listens
and... ... listens.

Nikki says no one listens better
than Great Bumbleduke the Third.

CHAPTER THREE

NIKKI'S WORST DAY EVER

One day, Nikki is walking home from school. It is quieter than usual because there are no seagulls in the sky.

Nikki walks down to the bridge across the stream.

The stream is full of beautiful, colourful, glistening fish. Some race each other between the tall, green reeds and some swim together in smaller, slower groups, enjoying the hazy, afternoon sun.

Nikki crosses the bridge and walks to the vegetable patch where her Mum is busy beside the carrots.

"Mum," says Nikki, "can we talk?
I've had - the - worst - day - ever!
Today was—"

Nikki's Mum isn't listening.

"Oh, you poor thing. That is such a pity.
Can we chat about it later? I'm shampooing Kitty."

Nikki leaves her Mum with her cat and her carrots and goes up to her room. She picks up her goldfish's bowl and sits on the edge of her bed.

"Oh, Great Bumbleduke the Third.
I've had - the - worst - day - ever!
Today was P.E.
Normally, I love P.E.

You know I swim like I'm a mermaid
diving deep for sparkly things.
You know I run like I'm a kangaroo
whose feet are tied to springs.

But today we got a new P.E. teacher...
Miss Leecher.

Her shout is so loud, it sounds like a monster roaring,
it shakes the ceiling and puts cracks in the flooring.

'Nikki!' yells Miss Leecher. *'You don't even try.*
I've seen legless lizards that can jump that high!
Why don't you try harder, Nikki? Nikki, tell me why?'

When Miss Leecher yells at me
I'm sometimes scared I'll..."

Great Bumbleduke the Third listens and then blows out two tiny bubbles.

BUP BUP

CHAPTER FOUR

ARRRRRRRRRRRRRRRRRRRRRRRRRRRRRRGH!

When the animals disappear, the seagulls are the first to go.

A different animal disappears every night.

The next to go are all of the dogs
then the pigs, bees, bears, hares, seals, eels, frogs, baboons, raccoons, ponies, pythons, gnats, rats, bats, sheep, cows, and then...

...the cats.

When Nikki's Mum finds out Kitty is missing, she says,

"Arrrrrrrrrrrrrrrrrrrrrrrrrrrrrrrrrgh!
This has gone too far!
My whole world is at its end.
I have lost my only friend..."

Nikki gasps and points to the floor.

"Mum. Please.
What are these?"

Out from the door, across the bridge and into the deep, dark forest, are big, clawed footprints. The footprints are wet and smell of salty water.

"Nikki!" gulps her Mum. "Whose are these feet?
They're not the feet of any 'thing' I'd want to meet.
They're big. They're clawed. Oh, don't tell me that
some slimy, grimy, monstrous 'thing' came here...

...and *ate* my cat?

Arrrrrrrrrrrrrrrrrrrrrrrrrrgh!"

"Come on, Mum. That can't be true. Can it?"

Nikki's Mum's face looks like a water balloon so full it is ready to burst.

"Mum, you don't think this... 'thing'... would eat... a *goldfish*... do you?"

"Oh, Nikki... I bet this 'thing' likes eating goldfish *best*."

"No!" screams Nikki. "Not Great Bumbleduke the Third! Not Great Bumbleduke the Third! Not Great Bumbleduke the Third!"

Nikki races to the top of her stairs, up to her bedroom, throws open the door and... in the middle of her room, in the middle of her bed, in the middle of his bowl, Great Bumbleduke the Third is... safe.

Nikki flings her arms around his bowl.

"Oh! I am never going to leave you again. I promise."

Whilst her Mum is busy weeping and wailing, Nikki doesn't let go of Great Bumbleduke the Third's bowl once. When it's time for sleep, Nikki takes the bowl to bed. Before she turns off the light, she whispers to her friend,

"You don't miss Kitty, do you?
Is it bad for me to say
in some ways things are *better*
since Kitty... went away?

I hated Kitty watching you
with such hungry looks
and stretching out her claws
like they were fish-catching hooks.
The last thing I want
is for Mum to be sad,
but I... don't... miss Kitty.
Does that make me... *bad*?"

Great Bumbleduke the Third listens and then blows out one tiny bubble.

BUP

Nikki nods, wraps her arms tight around his bowl, pulls up her covers and soon falls asleep.

CHAPTER FIVE

IN THE MIDDLE OF THE NIGHT

Wind whistles.
Grass rustles.
A door squeaks.
A step creaks.

Up the stairs, pitter-patter,
sounds like claws' clatter,
sounds like ripped cloth,
sounds like drip-drop-drip-drop... drip...

"Mum? Are you there?"

Silence.

"Mum? Is that you?"

Nikki can still feel the bowl between her arms. She turns on the light and looks down to the floor.

Clawed footprints lie between her bed and open door.

Nikki pulls back her covers.

The bowl is... empty.
The fish is... gone.

"Mum! Mum!"

Nikki leaps across the hallway to her Mum's closed bedroom door.

"Mum! Mum! Wake up! Wake up!"

From behind the door, she can hear her Mum gently snoring.

Across the hall, clawed footprints lead downstairs.

All Nikki knows for sure is that her fish has gone. He might still be alive. She must follow the footprints. She is going to bring him back!

Nikki quickly dresses. Clutching the empty bowl, she goes down to the kitchen. From the kitchen cupboard, she grabs some fish food. Great Bumbleduke the Third will definitely be hungry when she finds him.

She might be hungry, too. Nikki goes outside to the vegetable patch and pulls up some carrots.

Goldfish bowl. Fish food. Carrots. Nikki is sure she has everything she will need.

Step by step by step, Nikki follows the footprints out of the garden and to the bridge.

All the fish in the stream have gone.

Furious, Nikki crosses the bridge and follows the footprints deep into the night and deep, deep, deep into the dark forest...

CHAPTER SIX

YOU MUST STAY AWAY FROM RED ROCK ISLAND

Nikki follows the footprints out of the forest to a narrow beach.

Sunk into the sand are more clawed footprints.

They point out to sea, to a jagged island of blood red rock.

Everyone knows you must stay away from Red Rock Island.
All the adults say you must stay away from Red Rock Island...

...Nikki dives into the sea.

She swims faster than she has ever swum before, but she can hear Miss Leecher's voice inside her head.

'Why don't you try harder, Nikki?'

"I always try," thinks Nikki.
"I swim like I'm a mermaid, Miss Leecher."

Icy water slaps her, as big and heavy as polar bears' paws. The crashing waves feel as sharp as penguins' pointed, pecking beaks, but she must keep going. Just a few more strokes and...

and...

...Nikki pulls herself out of the freezing ocean and collapses on the red rock beach.

She is safe.

CHAPTER SEVEN

WHY YOU MUST STAY AWAY FROM RED ROCK ISLAND

By the midnight light of a full, round moon, Nikki sees the clawed footprints lead between piles of bones, all covered in teeth marks.

Whose are the teeth marks on these bones?
Why did she come here all alone?
Why didn't she stay with Mum back home?
Wait!

What’s that sound?

Clump. Clump. Clump. Clump.
The ground begins to quake.
Clump. Clump. Clump. Clump.
Nikki starts to shake.
Thump. Thump. Thump.
Nikki fears her heart may burst.
She looks across the beach, but...

...some ‘thing’ sees her first.

A slimy, grimy, monstrous ‘thing’ with claws like steel.

It *is* real.

A giant Troll comes crashing forward.
It chuckles with horrible glee.
It wears a thick, rope necklace.
On that necklace is a key.

The Troll bellows down at Nikki,

"WHO... ARE... YOU...?"

“I am Nikki. Have you got my fish, Troll?”

"YOU ARE FOOD!
NEW FOOD WHO'D
TASTE GOOD STEWED!"

A clawed hand reaches towards Nikki. She jumps to the side. Nikki moves as fast as a kangaroo whose feet are tied to springs.

"NAUGHTY FOOD
SPOILS MY MOOD!
THAT'S SO RUDE!"

The Troll crashes forward and the whole ground shudders. It knocks Nikki over.

SMASH!

Nikki drops the bowl. Broken glass flies everywhere.

Monstrous fingers, thick as snakes, close around her. Holding Nikki in its fist, the Troll carries her to a spiral, stone staircase leading beneath the ground. There is no escape as the Troll takes Nikki down, down, down to the deep, dark depths below Red Rock Island...

CHAPTER EIGHT

DEEPER. DARKER.

Deeper. Darker. Deeper. Darker.
Noises rising from below.
Deeper. Darker. Deeper. Darker.
Noises rising from below.

Squawking. Barking. Oinking. Buzzing.
Slurping. Scuttling. Chirruping. Ribbeting.
Shrieking. Bleating. Mooing. Meowing.
Animals howling.
Animals growling.
Noises rising from below.

If Nikki spoke Sheep,
she would know these bleats meant,
"Help! - Oh! - Help! - Oh!"

If Nikki spoke Cow,
she would know how moos meant,
"Let us go! Let us go!"

If Nikki could speak Seagullese,
she would understand these pleas,

"Liam? Look who's here, old chap!
Will you save us from this trap?"

Deeper. Darker. Deeper. Darker.
Noises rising, all around.
Noises rising, all around.
Noises rising, all around.

CHAPTER NINE

NIKKI'S WORST NIGHT EVER

As her eyes get used to the murky gloom, Nikki stares around this huge, underground room. It is full of cages.

In these cages she sees dogs,
pigs, bees, bears, hares, seals, eels, frogs,
baboons, raccoons, ponies, pythons, gnats, rats, bats,
sheep, cows, seagulls, but...

...no goldfish. No Great Bumbleduke the Third.

Nikki is hurled inside a tiny, metal cage. The Troll sticks one finger up inside its hairy nostril and plucks out a single, snotty nose hair. The nose hair looks like a long, curly worm. The Troll uses the nose hair to tie up Nikki, then slams her cage door shut and stomps out of the dungeon.

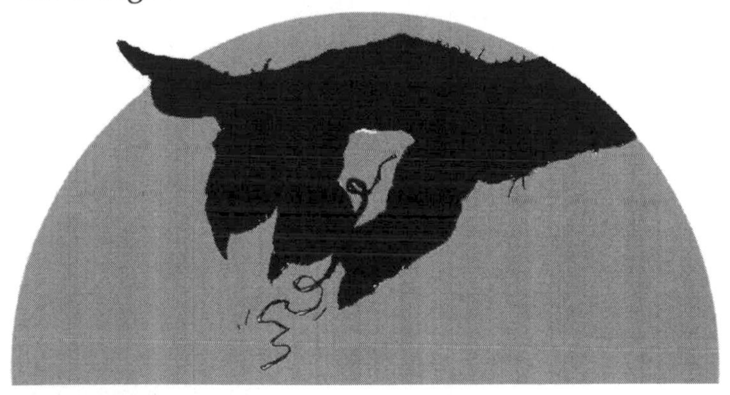

"Mew!"

There is Kitty, inside a cage. She presses her small, furry paw against her cage door. There is Kitty, but no Great Bumbleduke the Third.

"Oh! Kitty," calls Nikki, "I can't save you tonight.
I'm not good enough. Miss Leecher is right.
I am *not* as fast as a kangaroo.
I am slower than a swimmer
in a lake full of glue.
I am slower than a one legged ant
who's come down with the flu.
That Troll is going to eat us, Kitty...
and there is nothing I can do."

The Troll returns, carrying an enormous, iron cooking pot. A pot big enough to cook a girl in. From the rope necklace it removes the key and turns towards one of the cages.

Not Nikki's cage.

Kitty's cage.

"Mew!"

If Nikki spoke Cat,
she would know that mew meant,
"Nikki! Heeeeelp!"

The key goes into the lock of Kitty's cage door.

Nikki cries out,

"Stop! Don't eat Kitty! I've got other food.
Would you like a carrot?"

No reply.

"Maybe you don't like carrots.
Do you like fish food?"

The key turns in the lock of Kitty's cage door.

"Stop! Please! Eat me instead."

Silence.

All of the animals hush, as if they understand what Nikki is saying.

"Eat me. I'm bigger. It's a fact that
everyone knows people taste better than cats."

The key comes out. The Troll's hand moves away from Kitty's cage and towards Nikki. The key goes into the lock on Nikki's cage. The key turns. The door opens. The hand reaches in.

From above her, Nikki hears

CAW CAW CAW

If Nikki could speak Seagullese she would know that bird was saying,

"Oh my goodness, Noel, look here.
This brave young lady shows no fear."

His friend replies,

"Liam, that quite splendid girl's
the bravest person in the world!"

Nikki is ready.

Whilst she has been talking, Nikki has been rubbing the nose hair against a rough metal bar on the cage.

The nose hair snaps.

Nikki punches the Troll's giant finger.

"BWA HA HA HA HA!"

The Troll laughs and raises Nikki by her arm to its slobbering mouth. She feels Troll breath upon her, warm as sour milk.

Nikki lashes out with her foot and kicks the Troll's nose.

"BWA HA HA HA HA!"

The Troll moves Nikki closer to its big, sharp teeth.

Nikki throws a fistful of fish food into the Troll's face.

"ARRRRRRRRRRRRRRRRRRRRRRRRRRRRRGH!"

The fish food stings the Troll's tender eyes. It drops Nikki and the key. Nikki is falling... falling...

She catches the key!

Nikki now moves faster than any kangaroo (even one wearing a thousand springs). Dodging the Troll's stamping feet and waving arms, she races to the cages.

The first thing she does is free Kitty. Kitty takes the key in her mouth and scampers up to the highest cages. She frees all the animals too high for Nikki to reach. Kitty drops the key down to Nikki so she can open the lower cage doors.

The moment they are free, the seagulls take command.

"Attention, troops! Listen to Noel.
Together, we can beat this Troll.

All right! You bees, go sting its nose.
You lovely sheep, you chew its toes.

You gorgeous rats have whip-like tails,
so strike its hands and fingernails.

We'll beat this beastly Troll, all right.
We seagulls never lose a fight.

Chaaaaaaaaaaaaaaaaaaaaaaarge!"

The Troll lashes out with its fists and feet at the stampeding animal army. Above the shrieking, bleating and mooing, Nikki hears another sound.

BUP BUP

Great Bumbleduke the Third?

BUP

It's definitely him. Nikki would recognise the sound of his bubbles anywhere.

BUP BUP BUP

"Mew!"

Kitty bumps against Nikki's leg and points her paw towards a door, almost hidden between two cages. The door is too small for the Troll, but just about big enough for Nikki. It is from behind this door that Great Bumbleduke the Third can be heard.

BUP BUP BUP

Nikki picks up Kitty and runs past the Troll, past the fighting animals and dives through the door.

CHAPTER TEN

A FISH OUT OF WATER

On the other side of the door is a strange, little room made completely from red rock. There is a bed made from rock, a tiny, rock sink with a single, square tap, a pile of chipped rock toy soldiers and dolls and a round, rock bowl.

BUP BUP

It *is* him! Nikki runs forward to hug the bowl.

"Stop!"

Out from the shadows steps a girl... a young, Troll girl. She is about half the height of Nikki. Her face is fierce and her claws like tiny knives.

"Who are you? Why have you come
and caused such trouble for my Mum?"

Kitty runs for cover. Nikki takes a deep breath.

"I'm Nikki. Give my fish to me."

"No. You set my animals free.
All that work... it took me ages,
getting them in all those cages."

"*You* caught the animals?" Nikki laughs.
"You're so... *small*.
I don't believe
you caught them all."

"Shut up!" snaps the Troll girl.
"I am as big as... a hurricane
that never, ever quits."

The Troll girl picks up the rock bed. She balances its great weight on just one finger raised above her head.

Nikki puts her hand in her pocket, but she has used all the fish food. Her pocket is empty.

The Troll girl shrieks,

"I'm as strong as a tidal wave
the second that it hits!"

She flicks the rock bed down to the ground. Nikki staggers back as stones shatter and slap her skin.

"I swim quicker than the
boiling lava a volcano spits.
I run faster than an earthquake
that can rip the ground to bits."

Just then, one of the seagulls pokes its head out from the door.

"Quick! Our foe's so awfully strong.
We can't keep fighting for too long!"

All Nikki hears is

CAW CAW CAW

but she understands what the seagull is saying.

The Troll girl steps over the bits of broken bed and picks up the bowl.

"No!" pleads Nikki.

Too late. The Troll girl flips the water out of the bowl.

Out flies Great Bumbleduke the Third. He spins higher and higher until he nearly touches the ceiling, before he begins to fall.

Nikki hurls herself forward. She dives towards her falling friend, her arms outstretched.

Great Bumbleduke the Third flops down into her hands. Water sprays everywhere.

Nikki stands shakily, carefully cupping her fish. As the last drops of water drip from Nikki's hands, Great Bumbleduke the Third wriggles and flaps.

He can't breathe.

Tears begin to fill Nikki's eyes.

"You evil Troll. You know a fish needs water.
He's dying now because of what you've done,
but you don't care. You Trolls just slay and slaughter.
You evil Troll. You know a fish needs water.

You've got a Mum who listens to her daughter.
Who'll listen to me now? I'll have no one.
You evil Troll. You know a fish needs water
He's dying now because of what you've done."

Nikki cries.

The Troll girl stares at Nikki and then snorts,

"Shut up!"

The Troll girl snatches Great Bumbleduke the Third and takes him over to the tiny, rock sink. She turns on the tap and lets cool, clear water gently pour over him.

Great Bumbleduke the Third gasps.

BUUUP

The Troll girl looks at the fish in the sink and says,

> "All my Mum does, day and night,
> is bellow for more meat.
> She never listens to me.
> All she ever does is eat."

Great Bumbleduke the Third listens and then blows out one tiny bubble

BUP

The Troll girl fills the rock bowl with water and slides Great Bumbleduke the Third gently in.

She passes the rock bowl to Nikki, who hugs it tight.

"Without a fish to eat for tea
Mum's going to be so mad at me."

Great Bumbleduke the Third listens and then blows out five tiny bubbles.

BUP BUP BUP BUP BUP

Nikki looks at her fish, nods her head and picks up a piece of the broken rock bed. Its edge is thin and sharp.

Nikki sits on the floor and uses the sharp rock to cut into one of her carrots. The Troll girl watches, confused, as Nikki turns the carrot into something else. Layers of carrot peel away as Nikki carves. Kitty climbs into Nikki's lap and purrs as Nikki turns the carrot into a little carved carrot goldfish.

"You've seen our garden's veggie patch
with loads of carrots there to catch.
Come home with me. Let's do it now.
Let's make some fish. I'll teach you how."

The Troll girl cautiously opens the door back through to the dungeon.

"All right, but first you've got to come with me. We have to face my mum."

CHAPTER ELEVEN

WHAT DO YOU THINK?

"A-BOO-HOO-HOO... A-BOO-HOO-HOO..."

Surrounded by empty cages, the Troll mum weeps, alone.

"A-BOO-HOO-HOO... A-BOO-HOO-HOO..."

The Troll girl tiptoes forward and holds up the carved carrot goldfish to her mum. Her mum stops weeping.

"Go on. Try it, Mum."

Nikki hides the real Great Bumbleduke the Third behind her back.

"Shhh! Be quiet!" she tells him.

The Troll mum takes the carved carrot goldfish and nibbles at the edge.

"Well? Mum? What do you think?"

"THIS FISH IS... GOOD. NO BONES. NO SCALES.
NO SLIMY EYEBALLS OR TOUGH TAILS.
NOT HAD A FISH THIS GOOD BEFORE.
GO! GO! BRING MORE!"

CHAPTER TWELVE

HIGHER. LIGHTER.

Higher. Lighter. Higher Lighter.
Noises coming from above.
Higher. Lighter. Higher. Lighter.
Noises coming from above.

They sail home... all the dogs,
pigs, bees, hares, bears, seals, eels, frogs,
baboons, raccoons, ponies, pythons, gnats, rats, bats,
sheep, cows, cats...

...and seagulls. From high in the sky the seagulls call

CAW CAW CAW

which is Seagullese for

"Toodle-pip and cheerio!
Dear Nikki, you're our true hero."

Kitty rushes into the house and up onto Nikki's Mum's bed. Nikki's Mum gives a loud snore and Kitty begins to purr.

The Troll girl and Nikki stand on the bridge, looking down at the fish swimming safely back in their own stream.

Nikki thinks about the Troll mum, all those cages... and what it was like to be a prisoner and never free.

Nikki holds the rock bowl over the side of the bridge and turns it upside down.

Out flies Great Bumbleduke the Third.

He falls through the air and then...

Splash!

Nikki and the Troll girl watch as all the fish twirl and whirl in a magnificent fish dance that fills the whole stream with bubbles.

Great Bumbleduke the Third pokes his head out of the water, looks up at Nikki and opens and closes his mouth three times.

Anyone who didn't speak fish would just hear

BUP BUP BUP

but, as Nikki listens to Great Bumbleduke the Third, she knows exactly what he is saying.

PUZZLES

WICKED WORDSEARCH ONE

f	b	d	e	m	y	h	r	g	d
r	u	m	t	b	h	v	g	n	f
i	m	h	r	x	e	q	a	v	o
e	b	t	o	r	v	l	b	f	o
n	l	a	l	q	s	d	k	h	t
d	e	t	l	i	b	t	i	o	p
s	d	h	h	k	o	e	t	r	r
l	u	i	a	k	z	g	t	p	i
u	k	n	k	i	c	a	y	r	n
w	e	g	a	n	w	c	l	k	t

nikki
kitty
thing
troll
bumbleduke

footprint
island
cage
friends
rhyme

PUZZLES

CRAFTY CROSSWORD

Across:

1. It can be full and bright at night (4)
2. It crosses the stream (6)
5. The sound of seagulls (3,3,3)
6. The second animals to disappear (4)

Down:

1. Nikki swims like one (7)
2. The sound of a tiny bubble (3)
3. Trolls have sharp _ _ _ _ _ on their hands and feet (5)
4. Nikki moves as _ _ _ _ as a kangaroo (4)

WICKED WORDSEARCH TWO

y	t	y	w	t	k	b	o	w	l	t
g	o	m	p	c	e	y	r	h	y	k
o	r	w	o	i	s	a	w	j	b	e
l	r	r	t	w	e	n	c	s	h	y
d	a	s	p	l	a	s	h	h	s	x
f	c	m	u	s	o	t	e	l	e	t
i	e	b	u	b	b	l	e	s	a	r
s	m	m	h	l	c	c	l	m	g	q
h	m	e	d	b	o	a	t	c	u	l
o	f	e	o	h	p	c	l	q	l	a
f	o	o	d	p	g	z	f	b	l	e

goldfish	rock	seagull
bubbles	boat	teacher
bowl	food	splash
poem	carrot	key

ANSWERS

WICKED WORDSEARCH ONE

f	b	d	e	m	y	h	r	g	d
r	u	m	t	b	h	v	g	n	f
i	m	h	r	x	e	q	a	v	o
e	b	t	o	r	v	l	b	f	o
n	l	a	l	q	s	d	k	h	t
d	e	t	l	i	b	t	i	o	p
s	d	h	h	k	o	e	t	r	r
l	u	i	a	k	z	g	t	p	i
u	k	n	k	i	c	a	y	r	n
w	e	g	a	n	w	c	l	k	t

CRAFTY CROSSWORD

Across: 1. moon, 2. bridge, 5. caw caw caw, 6. dogs
Down: 1. mermaid, 2. bup, 3. claws, 4. fast

WICKED WORDSEARCH TWO

y	t	y	w	t	k	b	o	w	l	t
g	o	m	p	c	e	y	r	h	y	k
o	r	w	o	i	s	a	w	j	b	e
l	r	r	t	w	e	n	c	s	h	y
d	a	s	p	l	a	s	h	h	s	x
f	c	m	u	s	o	t	e	l	e	t
i	e	b	u	b	b	l	e	s	a	r
s	m	m	h	l	c	c	l	m	g	q
h	m	e	d	b	o	a	t	c	u	l
o	f	e	o	h	p	c	l	q	l	a
f	o	o	d	p	g	z	f	b	l	e